Praise for my other books

EGMONT

First published in Great Britain 2014
by Jelly Pie an imprint of Egmont UK Ltd
The Yellow Building, 1 Nicholas Road, London W11 4AN

Text and illustration copyright © Jim Smith 2014
The moral rights of the author-illustrator have been asserted.

ISBN 978 1 4052 7117 2

1 3 5 7 9 10 8 6 4 2

barryloser.com
www.jellypiecentral.co.uk
www.egmont.co.uk

A CIP catalogue record for this title is available from the British Library

Printed and bound in Great Britain by the CPI Group

57334/2

This book has been specially written and published for World Book Day 2014.
For further information, visit www.worldbookday.com.

World Book Day in the UK and Ireland is made possible by generous sponsorship from
National Book Tokens, participating publishers, authors and booksellers.

Booksellers who accept the £1 World Book Day Book Token bear the full cost of redeeming it.

World Book Day, World Book Night and Quick Reads are annual initiatives designed to encourage
everyone in the UK and Ireland - whatever your age - to read more and discover the joy of books.

World Book Night is a celebration of books and reading for adults and teens on 23 April,
which sees book gifting and celebrations in thousands of communities around the country:
www.worldbooknight.org

Quick Reads provides brilliant short new books by bestselling authors to engage adults in reading:
www.quickreads.org.uk

I am ~~not~~ nit a Loser

GIVE
A BUG
A HUG!

Barry Loser

Smellchecked by Jim Smith

AmazeKeel news

Probably the most exciting millisecond in the history of my whole entire life on earth amen was the other day after school when my mum called me into the kitchen.

'Look at this!' she said, holding up the Mogden Gazette. 'Feeko's Supermarkets are bringing out a new shampoo and they're looking for three kids to be in the advert! You could audition with Bunky and Nancy!'

BE A STAR!

excited nose

I jumped in the air and did a dance, and my trousers fell down. Then I picked up the phone and dialled my best friend Bunky's number, which I'm jealous of because it's better than mine.

makes nice pattern →

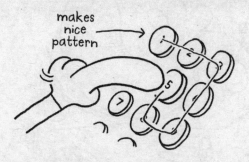

'Bunky! Have you heard?' I screamed when he answered.

'What, have I heard your VOICE?' said Bunky, cracking up at his own stupid joke, but I just ignored him and carried on with what I was saying.

'No you complete loseroid, they're auditioning for a shampoo advert at Feeko's tomorrow!' I snortled, almost weeing myself with excitement.

Bunky

me

I was jiggling around the kitchen like my mum when she dances to the radio, probably because I actually did need a real-life wee really badly.

'Keel!' said Bunky, which is what me and Bunky say instead of 'cool', mostly because it's keeler, but also because it's what they say in our favourite TV show, Future Ratboy.

Future Ratboy

his sidekick, Not Bird

I hung up on Bunky and dialled Nancy Verkenwerken's number, which I'm also jealous of, but not as much as Bunky's.

'Nancy! Have you heard?' I said when she answered, except it wasn't Nancy, it was her dad.

'Nancy's round at Bunky's,' said Mr Verkenwerken, so I hung up and phoned Bunky again, jealous of his number AND because Nancy was there.

the wee wiggle

loserish phone cord

'WHAT'S NANCY DOING ROUND YOUR HOUSE WITHOUT ME?' I shouted when Bunky answered the phone, except it wasn't Bunky, it was Nancy.

'I popped in. I do live next door to him, you know,' said Nancy, but I just ignored her and carried on with what I was saying.

Nancy
(obviously)

'Yeah, well, did he tell you the amazekeel news?' I said, stretching the phone cord so I could go for a wee in the toilet, which was across the hall from where I was standing in the kitchen.

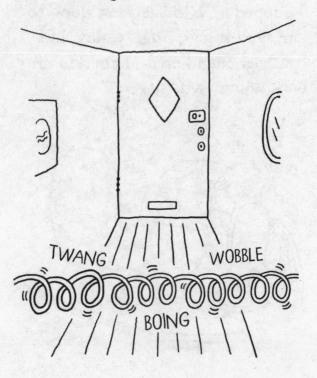

'Yeah, it's keel!' said Nancy, completely copying what me and Bunky say.

Suddenly and boringly my mum walked down the hall, carrying a pile of dirty washing. 'Arrrggghhh!' she screamed, tripping over the phone cord.

TRIP!

STRETCH

The phone flew out of my hand and I twizzled round like a ballerina. 'See you at Feeko's tomorrow morning. Eight o'clock sharp!' I shouted, wee going everywhere, not that I cared, because I was going to be in a shampoo advert!

Best mood ever

The next morning I sprang out of bed like there was a spring springing me out of it. I looked at the mattress and saw a massive spring springing out of the sheet and realised that a real-life spring had actually sprung me out.

like the phone cord

I chuckled to myself, jumping into the shower with a spring in my step, thinking how it was the first day of spring, which is my favourite season ever, even though I hate the word 'spring' and try not to say it all that much if possible.

SHHHHHHHHH

shower trying to stop me singing

Feeko's shampoo

'What's going on here?' said my mum when I came downstairs with my hair all washed and shiny. I think she was a bit surprised, seeing as I usually only have about one shower every eight million years.

'I have to look my best for the shampoo advert!' I said, and my mum did her smile she does when she thinks I'm the best son ever, which I am.

best
son
ever

'Ooh my snuggly little Snookyflumps!' she warbled, giving me a cuddle, which I wriggled out of even though I secretly quite liked it.

Then I skateboarded off to Feeko's Supermarket, going extra fast because of all the excitement-turbo-blowoffs I was doing.

What a lovely day

'Barry!' shouted Bunky as I skateboarded up to Feeko's playing it keel times a billion and three-quarters. He was halfway down the queue of kids, which was caterpillaring round the building like one of those long wriggly insect things I can never remember the name of.

'You made it!' I smiled, my hair glistening in the sunshine. Nancy strolled up and picked a flower that was growing out of a crack in the pavement, and I gave her a triple-reverse-upside-down-salute, which is what I do when I'm in the best mood ever.

sort of like the mattress spring

'Lovely day, isn't it!' she beamed, sniffing on the flower and sneezing into my face. The sun was beaming in the sky even more than Nancy, and Bunky pulled out a pair of **Future Ratboy** sunglasses.

built-in antennae

completely keel

how did they fit in pocket?

'Oh. My. Days. I am LUVVING your shades, Bunky!' said an annoying voice from behind me that sounded just like Sharonella's from our class at school.

I turned round and did a blowoff out of shock, because it actually WAS Sharonella, not that I should have been all that surprised, seeing as the voice had sounded EX-ACK-ER-LY like hers.

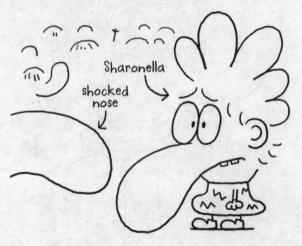

Sharonella

shocked nose

'Helloooooooo, Darren fans!' said
Darren Darrenofski, who I hadn't
spotted because he was standing
behind Sharonella, and I did
another blowoff because of
how annoying he is too.

Darren

crocodile
face

can of
Fronkle

'Next five kids!' shouted a spotty
fat man holding a clipboard,
and we shuffled into Feeko's
Supermarket, me first because
I'm the best.

The store room

'This way,' shouted the clipboard man, walking us through Feeko's, which was full of grannies and grandads doing their boring old Saturday morning shopping.

Right at the back of the store
was an enormous metal door with
a yellow poster on it saying 'Nit
Shampoo Auditions Here!'

'Nit shampoo? You didn't say
it was for NIT SHAMPOO!' said
Bunky, pointing at the poster and
then poking me in the nose with
the finger he'd just been pointing
at the poster with.

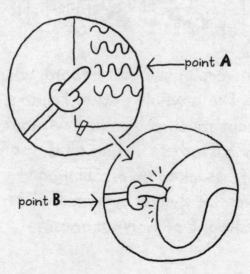

point **A**

point **B**

'Oh well, we're here now!' I smiled, thinking how I should be in a good mood more often, and I pushed the door open and walked through.

We were in the store room, which was like a whole nother Feeko's, except much colder and without any customers. It had all the same stuff stacked up in cardboard boxes, on shelves eight million times the height of normal ones.

The clipboard man walked us over to the shampoo aisle and told us to wait there, then walked off again, his footsteps echoing.

It was boring just standing there waiting, so I stuck my hand into a cardboard box and pulled out a bottle of Feeko's Cherry Shampoo.

I covered the 'SHAM' bit with my finger and put on my advert face. 'Mmm, Feeko's Cherry poo!' I snortled, and Bunky and Nancy weed themselves with laughter.

'That boy! The one with the hair!' growled a voice out of nowhere, and I spotted a man with an unlit cigar hanging out of his mouth, pointing at me. 'He's perfect!'

that man I was just talking about

I'm not used to people saying I'm perfect, so I jumped in the air and did a dance, and my trousers fell down. 'Little old keelness me?' I smiled, copying what **Future Ratboy** said when he won 'Keelest Person Ever' on the TV Awards last year.

The clipboard man walked over and bent down. 'The director would like to see you first,' he whispered in my ear, his voice going right through my brain and out the other ear, into one of Nancy's.

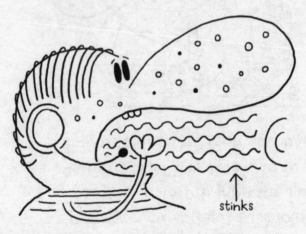

stinks

'What about me and Bunky?' Nancy said, looking all sad.

I looked over at my best friends and felt sorry for them for not being as brilliant as me.

'I don't go anywhere without these two!' I said and we walked over to the director together, me first again, because I'm the keelest, like I said earlier.

Feeko's Nit Shampoo

'Names?' said a frizzy-haired woman standing next to the director. Nancy and Bunky said their names, which are 'Nancy Verkenwerken' and 'Bunky' in case you didn't know.

'Barry Loser,' I said, smiling like I was in an advert for being Barry Loser.

'Barry Loser? That's hilarious!' chuckled the director, and everyone laughed, including Darren and Sharonella, who were standing at the edge waiting for their go.

clipboard man

I snortled, feeling like I was in one of those dreams where everything's going really well, and the frizzy-haired woman nudged us into the middle of the aisle.

'Just walk a bit, as if you're going down the street . . .' she said, looking at my hair all jealously.

I glanced at Bunky, who's sort of
like my pet dog, then at Nancy,
who's sort of like my pet cat,
which sort of made me their
leader, which meant I'd better say
something.

'Bunky, Nancy,' I said, putting my
arms round them, 'let's give this
a hundred and twenty million
billion percent!' I whispered,
copying what they say on my
mum's favourite TV talent show.
I put my hand up and we all high
fived, and it echoed round the
storeroom.

← high three
more like

Nancy started to stroll, twiddling her flower and looking up at the ceiling lights as if they were the sun. 'What a lovely day!' she beamed.

'Yes, isn't it glorious!' I said, glancing up at the fake sun and snatching Bunky's **Future Ratboy** sunglasses off his face. 'If only I didn't have these pesky nits in my hair . . .'

GRAB!

The director chuckled and the frizzy-haired woman jotted something down in her notebook.

'Can't . . . see . . .' mumbled Bunky, squinting from his no-sunglasses. He stumbled into a shelf and a cardboard box crashed to the floor, shampoo bottles flying everywhere.

'Hmmm . . .' grumbled the director, and the frizzy-haired woman jotted something else down in her notebook, but not in a good way. I bent over, worried Bunky was ruining everything, and picked up a bottle of almond conditioner.

pretending he's dead so I don't pick him up

'Ooh, Feeko's Nit Shampoo,' I said, totally making it up on the spot. 'Just the thingypoos for my nit problem!'

I flipped the lid open, held it
over my head and squeezed.
Light-brown slime drizzled on to
my hair and down my face.

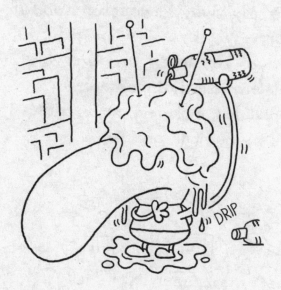

'Feeko's Nit Shampoo,' I said,
doing my best advert voice.
'Because it's keel!'

There was a millisecond of silence like you get in-between adverts on the telly, then the director stood up.

'Bravo!' he roared, and everyone in the whole shampoo aisle applauded, including me, because I'm my number-one fan.

Even more amazekeel news

After that we sat through seven billion other auditions, which were all completely rubbish, including Sharonella and Darren's.

Yay, shampoo!

Yeah, yay

Then the director whispered something into the frizzy-haired woman's ear and she clapped her hands, but not like she was clapping someone, more to shut us up.

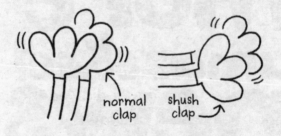

normal clap

shush clap

'Thank you all for coming today. It's been SO hard to decide!' she shouted, which is what they always say at things like this, just to make the losers feel better. 'However, the three winners have been chosen, and they are . . . Barry Loser, Nancy Verkenwerken and Bunky!'

You know how I said the most exciting millisecond in the history of my whole entire life on earth amen was when my mum told me about the shampoo auditions? That was until right now.

'YIPPEE-KEEL-KAYAY!' I screamed, jumping in the air with Nancy and Bunky, and we all did a dance, and my trousers fell down.

shampoo wiped off

A week later

It was a week later and my mum was dropping me, Bunky and Nancy off to film the advert.

'See you later for your big camping trip!' said my mum, because we were sleeping in the tent in my back garden that night to celebrate being famous.

'OK, Mrs Bunky!' I shouted, pretending she was Bunky's mum because of how embarrassing she is, and she ruffled my hair.

The advert was being filmed down the poshest street in Mogden, which was sort of like the shampoo aisle in Feeko's storeroom except the cardboard boxes were enormous houses, and instead of fake sun there was cloud.

Darren Darrenofski wobbled up, sipping on a can of Fronkle. 'Good mornkeels, Darren fans!' he burped, and I spotted something Sharonella-ish behind him.

'What in the name of unkeelness are YOU TWO doing here?' I said, patting my hair down where my mum had just ruffled it.

'We're spectatoring!' said Sharonella, and I felt sorry for them, not being the stars of a nit shampoo advert like me.

Darren's nose

Sharonella's whole head

my nose

The director walked over and ruffled my hair right where I'd just patted it down.

'Hey kids! I had the greatest idea for the advert last night,' he said, all excitedly. 'It's got everything. Energy, passion, FIZZAZZ!'

fizzazz

'What IS it?' said Sharonella, even though it was none of her business.

'One word: ROLLER SKATES!' he boomed, and I gulped, because I'd never roller skated in my life.

'That's two words,' said Nancy, and I trod on her foot to shut her up.

'One, two, what's the difference?' breathed the director, blowing a cloud of cigar smoke into my face.

mixed with
really bad
breath

FFFFFFFFF

I thought about my skateboard, and how roller skating is probably just like riding two skateboards instead of one.

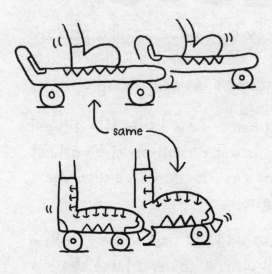

same

'Yeah Nancy, what's the difference?' I said, and she trod on BOTH my feet to shut me up.

Runaway Loser

Frizzy Hair gave us all a pair of roller skates and a helmet each. I put mine on and stood up.

You know how I said the advert was being filmed on the poshest street in Mogden? It's also the hilliest.

'Waaahhhh!!!' I screamed, rolling backwards down a huge slope.

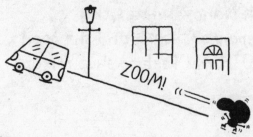

ZOOM!

'We have a runaway Loser,' said Clipboard Man into a walkie-talkie, and everybody laughed.

'Barrrryyyy!' cried Nancy, zooming after me on her roller skates, with Bunky right behind. They sped past and looped back, stretching their arms out and holding hands to catch me.

WHOOSH!

'Uunnggfh!' I blurted, crashing into them, and we all fell over.

I stood up wobblingly and patted my hair down for the eight millionth time that morning, even though it was inside a helmet. 'Let's film this advert!' I boomed, trying to sound like their leader, and I fell straight down on my bum again.

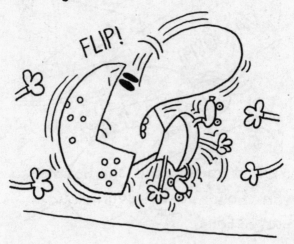

FLIP!

Action

'Aaaaaaannnnddd . . . ACTION!'
boomed the director, and Nancy
started to roller skate down
the road.

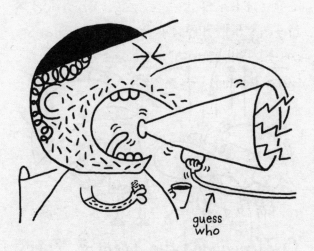

guess
who

'What a lovely day!' she beamed,
even though it was even cloudier
than before.

'Isn't it glorious!' I warbled, wobbling behind her, my arms waggling to keep steady. 'If only I didn't have these pesky nits doing poos all over my head . . .' I rolled past the camera and crashed into the frizzy-haired woman.

two seconds before crash

'CUT!' growled the director. 'Barry baby, where's the magic gone?' he said, blowing cigar smoke in my face AGAIN.

A huge black cloud had appeared behind him, and I imagined a giant director out in space, blowing cigar smoke on to the world.

the world

instead of moon

I tried to stand up, but my feet were skidding off in opposite directions. Bunky and Nancy rolled over and dragged me to the kerb. 'You OK, Barry?' said Nancy, and I gave her a thumbs up, mostly because I was too out of breath to speak.

'OK, let's go again,' shouted the director. 'Really work it this time, guys. Aaaaannnnddd . . . ACTION!'

'What a LUVVERLY day!' said Nancy, and Bunky twizzled round like a ballerina.

'Isn't it glorious!' I said, zooming past them and tripping over a camera wire. 'ARRGGHHH!!!' I screamed, flying through the air and landing in a bush.

'Maybe we could get rid of the roller skates?' I heard the frizzy-haired woman say to the director, her voice muffled from all the leaves around my ears.

The air had turned cold, like in the storeroom at Feeko's.

'What, and lose the FIZZAZZ?!' growled the director. He looked at his watch, then the big black cloud, and shook his head.

rain
o'clock

'Is there anyone else here who can roller skate?' asked the director.

'Me!' shouted Darren Darrenofski before I'd even clambered out of the bush.

LEAP!

Thunder and lightning

'Help me!' I wailed, trying to get up, my feet running away from their owner, who was me.

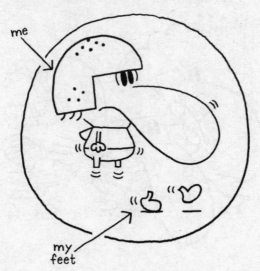

me

my feet

Darren was squidging his fat little feet into a spare pair of roller skates as Bunky and Nancy glided towards me. They grabbed a Barry-arm each and rolled me over to the director.

'You've got to give him one more chance!' said Nancy, holding me up like an old grandad who can't walk.

Lightning struck in the distance as Darren trundled past doing a little jump. 'Barry baby, what can I tell you,' sighed the director. 'I've gotta get this thing filmed before the rain starts. I'm sorry, really I am.'

RUMBLE

My knees gave way and I collapsed to the floor like an empty Feeko's carrier bag. 'But you said I was perfect!' I cried.

I lay on the ground, thinking how this whole auditioning thing had been my idea in the first place.

'BUNKY, NANCY, I ORDER YOU NOT TO BE IN THE NIT SHAMPOO ADVERT WITHOUT YOUR LEADER!' I roared, but in a nice way, and waited for them both to say 'OK' and take off their roller skates.

CRACK!

Bunky looked at me all guiltily, like a dog just before it's about to do a poo right in the middle of the pavement.

naughty Bunky

Nancy glided over, her ponytail swishing like a cat's tail. She held my hand in hers and looked me in the eyes, then glanced towards the director.

BZZZ—

'I'm so sorry, Barry,' she said,
turning round and floating away,
and I did the angriest blowoff in
the history of angry blowoffs ever.
Or maybe it was just the thunder.

The long walk home

It was a long walk home in the rain from the posh street to my house, especially with Sharonella bobbling along next to me for half of it, going on about how we were the only two people not in a nit shampoo advert.

'Forget about that lot, Barry. Who needs 'em, that's what I say!' she wheezed, huffing and puffing to keep up, but I just ignored her and carried on with what I was doing.

I was soaking wet by the time I got to my front door. 'What's happened to my Snookyflumps?' chuckled my mum as the clouds parted and the sun came out behind me.

I barged past her up to my bedroom and started packing my rucksack. 'Barrypoos, are you OK?' she warbled, her knees clicking as she climbed the stairs.

I grabbed my cuddly **Future Ratboy** and stuffed him into the bag, looking out the window at the tent that me, Bunky and Nancy were supposed to be camping in tonight, to celebrate being famous.

'Where are Bunky and Nancy?' said my mum, and I thought of them celebrating with Darren, somewhere else.

I swung the rucksack over my shoulder and stomped downstairs, straight towards the tent.

'SEE YOU IN A MILLION YEARS,' I shouted to everyone in the whole wide world, and I zipped the floppy door shut behind me.

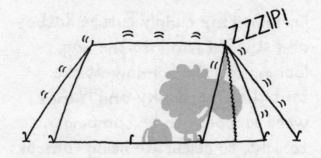

ZZZIP!

Camping on my ownypoos

I lay down on my sleeping bag and closed my eyes, trying to forget about it all, and felt something tickle my face.

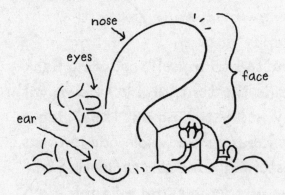

nose

eyes

ear

face

'ARRRGGGHHH! SPIDER!' I screamed, unzipping the door and rolling on to the wet grass. I scrabbled at my nose, which was where the tickle was, and a sleeping-bag feather floated off it, into the sky.

I tutted to myself, crawling back inside the tent, and lay down with my head sticking out like a dog in his kennel. The whole garden was glistening now, sun reflecting off the wet leaves and into my eyes.

One of those insect things with seven trillion legs trundled past, smiling. 'What are YOU so happy about?' I mumbled.

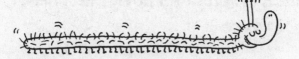

Three centimetres away an ant was busy dragging his dead ant-friend down a tiny little hole in the earth.

'You wouldn't abandon YOUR leader, would you, Mr Ant?' I whispered to him in my best insect voice.

I looked around at all the millions of other insects pottering about minding their own businesses and thought how sweet they were, eating leaves and doing the tiniest poos ever.

And then it hit me.

What had I been thinking, wanting to be in a Feeko's Nit Shampoo advert? I wasn't an insect murderer!

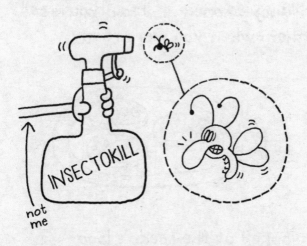

Who did Nancy and Bunky reckon they were, roller skating around with Darren Darrenofski, telling people to kill innocent little bugs!

'Snackypoos, Snookyflumps!'
chirped my mum, knocking on the
tent and passing me a plate of
chocolate digestives. 'Bunky and
Nancy phoned . . . I said you'd call
them when you were ready.'

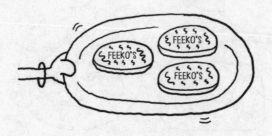

I looked at the Feeko's logo
stamped into the biscuits and
thought of my evil insect-killing
ex-best-friends with their
keeler-than-mine phone
numbers, starring in their
stupid nit shampoo advert.

'Fanks, Mumsy,' I said, taking a bite of one, and twelve billion crumbs scattered on to the grass. 'Who needs 'em!' I whispered in my insect voice, settling down to dinner with my millions of tiny new best friends.

Insect
murderers

All of a non-sudden it was Monday and I was skateboarding to school through Mogden Common, which is this massive bit of grass in the middle of town where everyone takes their dogs to do poos.

TREMBLE

A butterfly was flitter-fluttering next to my head like a miniature fan, his tiny wings cooling me off in the morning sun, when I spotted a worm wriggling across the pavement.

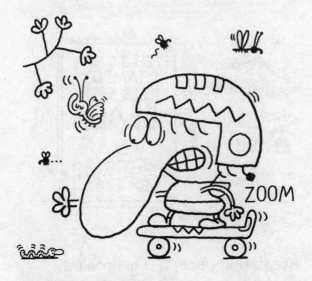

ZOOM

'EEEKK!' I shrieked, swerving to miss him and crashing nose-first into a billboard.

'FEEKO'S NIT SHAMPOO KILLS NITS DEAD!' said the headline on the poster. Underneath there was a photo of Bunky, Nancy and Darren roller skating down the road, looking all happy and nit-free.

'Insect murderers!' I grumbled, standing up, and a fly flew right into my eyeball, completely and utterly blinding me.

'Good!' I mumbled, because I didn't have to look at that stupid advert any more. Then I realised it wasn't good, because I'd accidentally killed a fly.

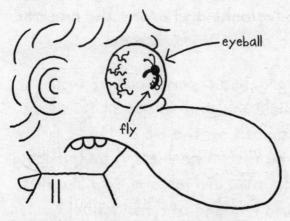

I rubbed my eye and looked into my hand. The fly was curled up, drowned in my tears, his little wings stuck to his body like my clothes after that walk home in the rain the other day.

'I'm sorry, Mr Fly,' I said, kneeling down and scraping a hole in the dirt. I plopped him in and put the dirt back, then picked up an old lolly stick that was lying on the pavement and broke the end off to make a gravestone.

I grabbed a pencil out of my rucksack and wrote 'FLY' in tiny capitals on the bit of wood. 'May you rest in keelness,' I said, digging the mini gravestone into the dirt and heading off for school.

Nits are the keelest

The annoying thing about being the nicest, most non-insect-killing person in the whole wide world amen is that you have to stop every two minutes to bury all the insects you keep accidentally killing.

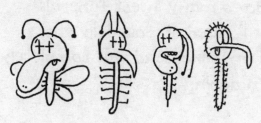

Like the ant I ran over with my
skateboard three seconds after I'd
drowned that fly in my eyeball.
And the daddy-long-legs I
swallowed while yawning eight
milliseconds after that.

By the time I got to school I'd had
to do so many insect funerals
that I'd used up four lolly sticks
and my pencil lead was completely
worn down.

There was a crowd around Bunky and Nancy as I walked through the classroom door. Everyone was asking them about the advert and whether they were millionaires yet.

walking through door (get it?) →

'Barry!' said Bunky, walking over to me all guiltily like a dog that's just done a wee in the middle of the living room carpet.

'How are you, Barry?' said Nancy, coming over and curling her arm round my shoulder, but I just ignored her and carried on with what I was doing.

'I had a word with the director about the next advert. He said we could do it on skateboards!' smiled Bunky, as if we were still best friends, and I mouthed 'Yay!' and waggled my hands all sarcastically.

doesn't realise I'm being sarcastic

sarcastic waggling

I flumped down at my desk and started drawing insects in my notebook. 'I don't want to be in your evil nit-murdering adverts,' I mumbled, writing 'NITS ARE THE KEELEST' in my best capitals at the top of a new page.

Just then, Darren barged through the classroom door on his roller skates. 'Helloooo, Darren fans!' he burped, holding up a phone and pressing play on the screen.

I squinted my eyes and saw him, Bunky and Nancy gliding down the posh street, high fiving each other and acting like they were the keelest people ever. 'FEEKO'S NIT SHAMPOO KILLS NITS DEAD!' growled a voice at the end of the advert, and everyone cheered.

'What are you cheering for? I shouted, scraping my chair and standing up. 'These people are murdering innocent nits!' I sat back down and drew a woodlouse, my hand shaking from how angry I was.

'He's gone stark raving bonkers!' laughed Darren, pressing play on the phone screen to make the advert start again. 'If anyone wants my autograph, I'm signing people's faces this lunchtime in the playground!'

A fly that'd been buzzing against the classroom window bonked his nose straight into the glass one last time and fell to the floor, dead from nose-bonk. I rolled my eyes, snapping a mini gravestone off a lolly stick in my pocket.

'Psst! Barry!' whispered Sharonella as I bent down to pick up the fly. 'I know you've gone mad and everything but I just wanted to say that I'm there for you, OK?'

I wasn't listening to her though. I was too busy coming up with one of my brilliant and amazekeel plans.

BZZZ ~

Give a bug a hug

The queue for autographs caterpillared all the way round the playground like one of those insects with twenty trillion legs I can never remember the name of.

'One at a time, Darren fans!' burped Darren, signing Fay Snoggles's nose, and Bunky snortled, scribbling his stupid name in someone's autograph book underneath Nancy's.

'Ready?' I said to Sharonella, taking a deep breath and accidentally breathing in a mosquito.

'Huh? Oh yeah, I was born ready!' said Sharonella, who was standing next to me picking her nose and holding a poster with 'NITS ARE PEOPLE TOO!' written on it.

I looked at my poster, which said 'GIVE A BUG A HUG' in my biggest capitals, patted myself on the back for coming up with such a brilliant and amazekeel idea, and started marching towards my ex-best-friends.

'Ban Feeko's Nit Shampoo!' I shouted, waving my poster in the air and hitting a ladybird but not killing it, so that's OK.

'GIVE-A-BUG-A-HUG,' burped Darren, reading my poster out loud. 'OK!' he snortled, running towards a daddy-long-legs that was flying past, minding its own business. 'Come to daddy, Daddy!' he snarfled, grabbing it by the wings and giving it a cuddle.

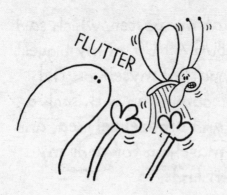

FLUTTER

'NOOO!!!' I screamed, dropping my poster and running towards him. Darren opened his arms and the daddy-long-legs dropped to the floor, all dizzy. 'You almost killed him!' I cried, stroking its wings, and it floated off, a bit wobbly.

'Oh no, I'm about to tread on an anty-want!' said Darren in a baby voice, lifting his foot above an ant that was strolling past. I scrabbled towards it on my hands and knees and scooped it up just in time.

The ground shook as Darren's foot stomped on to the floor, or maybe it was Mrs Dongle the school secretary bounding over.

'Boys, boys, I cannot tolerate this tomfoolery!' she wheezed, the wooden beads on her necklace knocking against each other.

'He started it!' burped Darren, opening a can of Fronkle and slurping it down in one go.

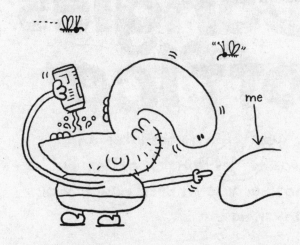

Mrs Dongle looked at me, lying on the floor holding an ant, then over at my poster. 'GIVE A BUG A HUG,' she said, reading it out loud. 'That's perfect!'

Mrs Dongle's office

It was ten minutes later and I was in Mrs Dongle's office, but not because I'd been naughty or anything.

'Have you heard about Mogden Common, Barry?' she smiled, offering me a chocolate digestive.

'Yes,' I said, but it came out as 'Mmf' because of the chocolate digestive I'd just stuffed in my mouth. 'It's that bit of grass where all the dogs do their poos,' I mumbled, spraying crumbs all over her desk.

Mogden Common

'That's it!' she chuckled. 'It's one of the last natural parts of Mogden left. Did you know that Feeko's wants to build a brand new mini supermarket right in the middle of it?' she said, suddenly all serious.

I thought of Mogden Common and remembered Mr Fly, lying in his tiny grave. 'I HATE Feeko's,' I said, looking out the window at Bunky and Nancy acting all keel because of their stupid Feeko's advert.

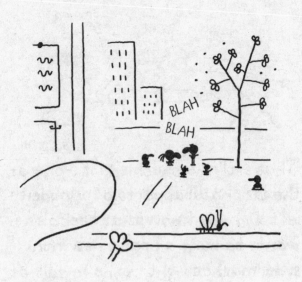

'There's a protest march coming up to stop them building it,' said Mrs Dongle, passing me another digestive, and I started to realise why the ground shook when she ran. 'Your posters would add just the FIZZAZZ we need!'

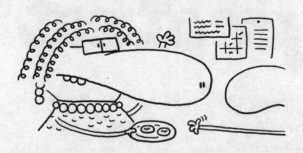

I slotted the biscuit into my mouth like a coin into a vending machine, and a blowoff popped out the other end.

The Feeko's protest

I spent the whole rest of the week making posters for Mrs Dongle, and burying insects I'd accidentally killed, and not telling Sharonella about the Feeko's protest, otherwise she'd want to come too.

Then all of a non-sudden it was Saturday and I was standing on the edge of Mogden Common with Mrs Dongle and all her wooden-bead-necklace friends and their husbands, wondering how in the unkeelness my life had ended up so loserish.

'Boo Feeko's!' growled an old granny, doddering past with a pram full of sausage dogs. She pulled a tied-up plastic bag out of her pocket and threw it at the enormous billboard that had been put up the day before.

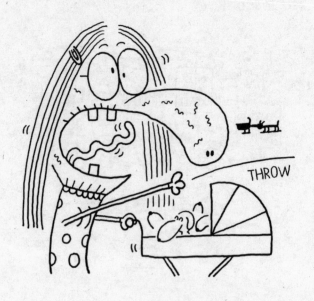

THROW

'YOUR NEW FEEKO'S FUNSIZE WILL BE HERE SOON!' said the billboard in the biggest capitals ever, and I wondered if me and Mrs Dongle's friends were wasting our time with our tiny little posters.

'Yes, that's right, Boo Feeko's!'
shouted Mrs Dongle, waving her
poster. On it I'd written 'FEEKO'S
IS FOR LOSERS', which wasn't my
most genius idea ever, but she
seemed to like it.

A van with a satellite dish on the
roof and 'Mogden TV' written on
its side screeched up. A man with
a camera jumped out, followed
by a lady with blonde hair and a
microphone.

'We are live at Mogden Common, where a riot has broken out in protest against the new Feeko's Funsize!' she said, flicking her fringe like me when I had my bouncy hair for the audition.

I looked around at all the Mrs Dongles and their husbands, standing there eating sandwiches and drinking tea, and wondered if this was what being in a riot was like.

Over on the other corner of the common, three figures started to glide towards us. One looked like a dog crossed with a human, the other had a cat's tail growing out of her head, and the third was half crocodile, half fat little belly.

I zoomed my eyes in and realised it was Bunky, Nancy and Darren, out practising their roller skating for the next evil nit-killing shampoo advert.

GLIDE

The cameraman swivelled round and started to film. 'This is verrry interesting,' said the blonde lady. 'It seems the stars of the huuugely successful Feeko's Nit Shampoo advert have turned up. Who knows what could happen next?'

What happened next

'It's those nit shampoo kids!'
shouted the old granny, giving
her pram a push and letting go.

It zoomed off like me on roller
skates, slicing a worm in half with
one of its wheels. 'Get 'em, boys!'
she cackled, and the dogs leaped
out of the pram and ran towards
Bunky like a string of sausages.

'ARRGGHHH!!!' screamed Bunky,
who's COM-PER-LEET-ER-LY scared
of dogs. He twizzled round to
zoom off and fell straight down
on his bum. The sausage dogs
swarmed round him, wagging their
tails and yapping.

not really
a sausage

YAP!

WAG!

Mrs Dongle dropped her poster
and bounded over. 'Bad doggies,
naughty pooches!' she warbled, the
TV people right behind her.

'Tell us how you're feeling!' said the blonde lady, stuffing her microphone into Bunky's face.

'My bum hurts,' said Bunky, a sausage dog licking his face.

I tiptoed over and watched from behind my poster, hoping they wouldn't see me.

'Well, well, if it isn't Barry Loser!' burped Darren, spotting me straight away, probably because of my massive nose sticking out from behind the poster. 'How many ants have you snogged today?' he laughed.

new helmet

DAZZER!

The camera swung round to me and I felt myself go the colour of a bottle of Feeko's Cherry Shampoo.

'How many have you KILLED, insect murder?' I shouted, waving my poster and hitting a daddy-long-legs but not killing it, so that's OK.

'None yet, but it's never too late!' said Darren, grabbing a fly that was flying past, and all the Mrs Dongles and their husbands gasped.

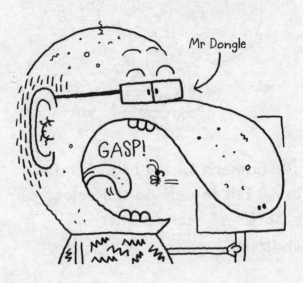

Mr Dongle

GASP!

'Truly shocking scenes here at Mogden Common,' said the blonde lady into the camera. 'That was one of the stars of the Feeko's Nit Shampoo advert happily murdering a fly, just for the fun of it. This is Sandy Sandals for Mogden News Tonight!'

Darren opened his hand and the fly flew off dizzily. 'Look! He's alive!' he shouted, but it was too late. Sandy Sandals and the cameraman were getting into their van and zooming off.

VROOM!

MOGDEN NEWS

113

The news

'Bazza, have you heard?!' screamed Sharonella as I skateboarded in through the school gates on Monday morning.

'What, have I heard your VOICE?' I said, chuckling to myself about my own joke, not that I was in much of a chuckling mood.

'No, the news about Darren!'

I flipped my skateboard up and took my helmet off, scratching my head because all of a sudden I'd been feeling a bit itchy.

SCRATCH

'Feeko's fired him!' snortled Sharonella. 'Nancy and Bunky too! They saw what Darren did on Mogden News and said they couldn't have insect murderers in their nit shampoo adverts!'

I was just about to do my
dance that makes my trousers
fall down, when I spotted Bunky
walking through the school gates
with Nancy and Darren.

'I suppose you're happy now,
aren't you,' mumbled Bunky all
sadly, scratching his head.

'Not really,' I mumbled back, because I wasn't really. I still hadn't been in a Feeko's Nit Shampoo advert, plus I didn't have any friends apart from Sharonella and the insects, not that they counted if I was being honest, which I was.

CLANG! CLONK! DONK! CLANK! CLUNK!

The sound of wooden beads clanging against each other floated into my ears and I span round and saw Mrs Dongle.

'Have you heard the news, Barry?'
she warbled, and I scratched my
head while shaking it. 'Our little
protest was a complete waste of
time. Didn't do anything! They're
still going to build that ghastly
Feeko's Funsize!'

BZZZ

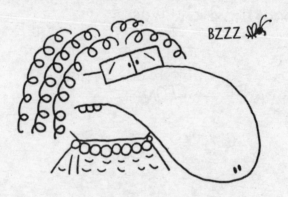

I did my sad face, mostly just
to make Mrs Dongle happy,
and carried on standing
there scratching my head.
And then it happened.

Nits

'ARRGGHHH!!! NITS!!!' screamed Mrs Dongle all of a sudden, pointing at my hair, and she jumped and ran off, her wooden beads clanging.

WAGGLE

'What is it? WHAT IS IT?' I cried, even though Mrs Dongle had said what it was.

Sharonella tiptoed over and peered into my hair. 'OH. MY. DAYS! Barry, you've got like a kazillion nits!' she said, squirming away from me and running off, screaming.

ZOOM!

I reached out to Nancy, forgetting
we weren't friends any more,
which is what happens when
you're too busy worrying about
all the nits eating away at your
brain.

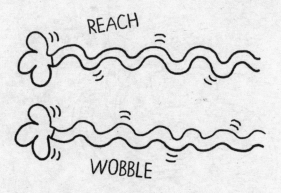

REACH

WOBBLE

'Nancy, you've got to help me!' I
wailed, my legs and arms flailing.

Nancy slinked away from me, scratching her head, and I zoomed my eyes in and spotted the most nit-looking thing I've ever seen going for a morning stroll along her eyebrow.

nit-looking thing

SCRATCH!

eyebrow

'ARRGGHHH!!! NITS!!!' I screamed, pointing at Nancy, and she started scratching and flailing, just like me.

'ARRGGHHH!!! NITS!!!' screamed Darren all of a sudden, pointing at Bunky's hair, and Bunky joined in with me and Nancy, itching himself like a dog.

'ARRGGHHH!!! NITS!!!' screamed
Bunky, pointing at Darren, and
that was how me, Bunky, Nancy
and Darren all ended up standing
in a circle doing the scratchy
nit dance.

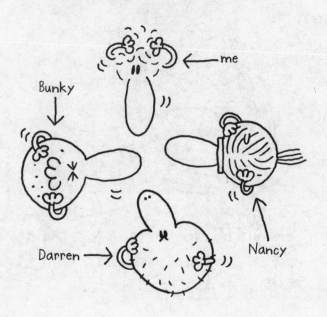

Nurse Nigel

It was ten minutes later and we were all in the nurse's room, but not because we had nits or anything.

'These aren't nits,' said the nurse, whose name is Nigel, tweezering one out of my ear and looking at it with a magnifying glass, all confused. 'They're fleas!'

I glanced over at Bunky, then Nancy, but not at Darren, because I don't really like looking at him all that much.

'The sausage dogs!' I laughed, remembering how one of them had been really scratching his bum with his mouth just before he'd licked Bunky's face.

Bunky's nose

flea

that dog

'Most extraordinary,' mumbled Nurse Nigel to himself. He opened his cupboard door and peered in, scratching his chin, but not because he had fleas or anything. 'Here we go!' he smiled, pulling out a big plastic bottle with 'Feeko's Flea Shampoo for Dogs' written on it in massive non-capitals.

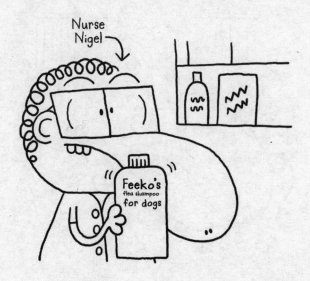

Nurse Nigel

So that's how I ended up in the
school showers with Bunky, Nancy
and Darren, stripped to my **Future
Ratboy** vest and pants and
covered in Feeko's Flea Shampoo
for Dogs.

Feeko's Flea Shampoo for Dogs

'Do us a favour Barry,' burped Darren, foam and dead fleas running down his belly. 'Next time she goes on a protest, tell your mum not to bring her sausage dogs!' he snortled, and Nancy and Bunky giggled, trying not to laugh out loud.

foam bubble

dead flea

'She's YOUR mum, not mine!' I shouted, looking down at all the dead fleas floating in the water and feeling a bit bad because I'd gone back to being an insect killer like my evil ex-best-friends.

'Get 'em, boys!' shrieked Nancy, doing her impression of the old granny with the pram, and I snortled to myself then stopped, because I was still angry with Bunky and Nancy for abandoning their leader.

looks like a toilet plunger taking off

'I'm sorry Barry, real-keely I am,' said Bunky, his whole head covered in flea shampoo foam. 'We shouldn't have done the advert without you.'

'Yeah, I don't know what came over us,' said Nancy, rubbing flea shampoo into her armpits. 'Pleeeaaassseee forgive us!' she groaned, staggering towards me with her arms stretched out like some kind of foam monster.

too much steam

'Yuck, I'm gonna be sick from all this niceness,' said Darren, and I looked at the three of them covered in flea shampoo and smiled, thinking how it would be keel if we were all in a Feeko's Flea Shampoo advert one day.

'What a LUVVERLY day!' I beamed, grabbing a handful of foam and squodging it on to Nancy's head.

'Isn't it glorious!' smiled Nancy, bonking me on the nose.

'Feeko's Flea Shampoo for Dogs!' said Bunky, picking up a handful of dead fleas and doing his best advert smile.

I put my arms round him and Nancy, and Darren too, because I was in a good mood all of a sudden.

'It's the keelest!' we all shouted, but we didn't jump in the air and do a little dance, because that's extremely dangerous when you're in or around water. Plus I didn't want my pants to fall down.

The endy-poos.

Name the dead bug!

(Just make them up)

- - - - - - - - -   - - - - - - - - -   - - - - - - - - -

- - - - - - - - -   - - - - - - - - -   - - - - - - - - -

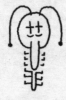

- - - - - - - - -   - - - - - - - - -   - - - - - - - - -

About the smellchecker

Jim Smith is the keelest kids' book smellchecker in the whole wide world amen.

He graduated from art school with first class honours (the best you can get) and went on to create the branding for a sweet little chain of coffee shops.

He also designs cards and gifts under the name Waldo Pancake.

'I'm really excited to be part of World Bok Day!' says Jim, misspelling 'book', which is embarrassing, seeing as he's also a spellchecker.

SNIFF

↑ this book

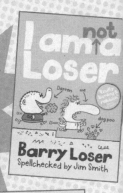

WORLD BOOK DAY *fest*

Want to **READ** more?

 Visit your LOCAL BOOKSHOP

- Get some great recommendations for what to read next

- Meet your favourite authors & illustrators at brilliant events

- Discover books you never even knew existed!

 WWW.BOOKSELLERS.ORG.UK/ BOOKSHOPSEARCH

 Join your LOCAL LIBRARY

You can browse and borrow from a HUGE selection of books and get recommendations of what to read next from expert librarians—all for FREE! You can also discover libraries' wonderful children's and family reading activities.

 WWW.FINDALIBRARY.CO.UK

GET ONLINE!

Visit **WWW.WORLDBOOKDAY.COM** to discover a whole *new* world of books!

- Downloads and activities
- Cool games, trailers and videos
- Author events in your area
- News, competitions and new books —all in a **FREE** monthly email